hello
grand
mamoon!

written by **Donna Steinmann**

illustrations by **Tamara Guion**

EARTHTIME PUBLICATIONS

In a great big city lived a little girl named Tula. Tula was sad. Her Grandma Nellie had died, and Tula missed her very much. She missed the comfort and warmth of Grandma Nellie's hugs and the smell of her wonderful cooking, but most of all Tula longed to hear her grandma's stories.

Whenever the moon was full, Grandma Nellie would read Tula's favorite story of all. Tula imagined herself nestled in her grandma's soft warm lap listening to her gentle voice tell of a time long, long ago.

"Thousands of years before you were born," Grandma Nellie began, "Village Earth was home to many small tribes of people. These ancient tribes had a magical way of seeing. The planets and stars of the night sky inspired their songs and storytelling. They especially liked to tell stories about the moon because, long ago, when the moon was full, our ancestors could see the face of a great round moon mother."

Gealach

Mamaki Menos

Mond

Maat   Moon

Mama Ogllo

Lua

La Luna

Kuu

Mother Mah

Ksiezyc

Inanna

Osiris
                    Tsuki
Yuet

Mirror of Maya   Selene

Wide Shining One

Peyyapi

Old Woman Who Never Dies

Dianna

Isis

Menulis

Great Mother

Mahina

Macha Alla

"Children from all over Village Earth celebrated the beauty of the great round moon mother. In the islands of the South Pacific the Polynesians called the moon 'Mahina'. They sang out to her and pounded on drums. Native Americans sat in circle and told stories of 'The Old Woman Who Never Dies'. The ancient Persians sang to Metra, 'The One Whose Love and Light Shines Everywhere'. In China they told stories of Chang Er, the goddess who fled to the moon to escape her cruel husband."

Ma

Metra

Astarte

Er

"Over time things began to change on Village Earth. Towns grew and grew until they became big cities. People became so busy that they forgot to look up. No one sang out the moon's ancient names any more. Children no longer danced or drummed out greetings to her. Eventually the moon's image became hidden behind tall buildings and bright city lights."

Always, at the end of the story, Tula tried to find the woman in the moon. "Look carefully, Tula, and one day you will see what our ancestors saw," Grandma Nellie told her. But Tula never could. And now, with her grandma gone, Tula had little hope that she would ever learn this magical way of seeing the moon.

But that night, as Tula gazed out of her bedroom window, thinking about her grandma, the big round yellow moon slowly began to rise over the rooftops and tall buildings. This time, something seemed different to Tula.

The moon looked so big and so close that Tula wanted to reach out and touch it. She pressed her nose right up to the window and tried hard to see the woman in the moon, but she could not.

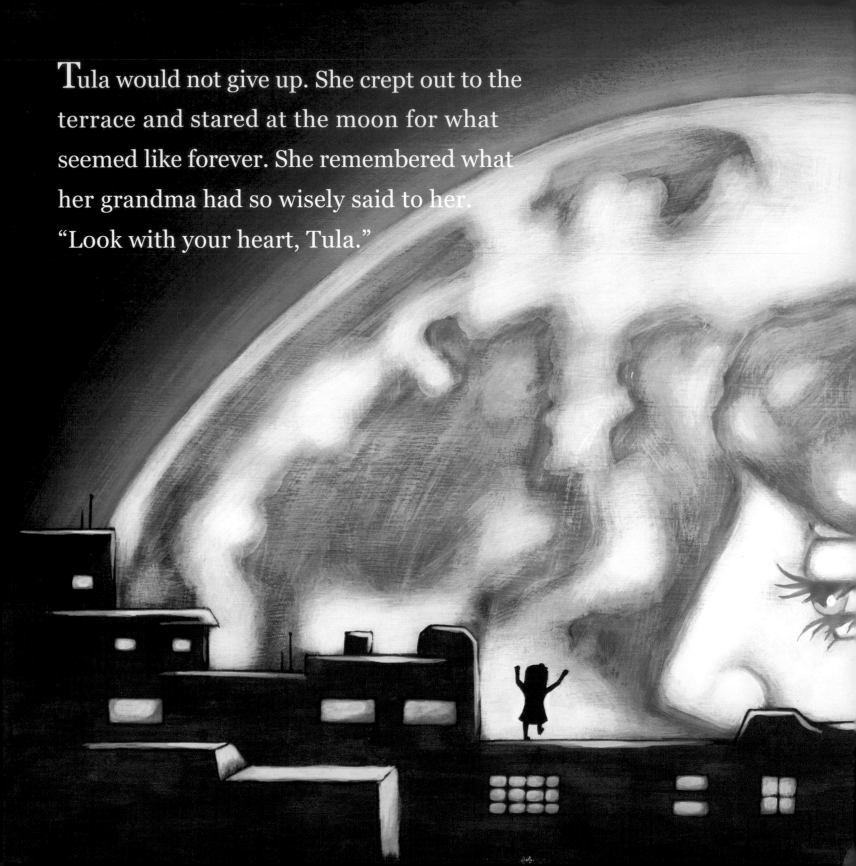

Tula would not give up. She crept out to the terrace and stared at the moon for what seemed like forever. She remembered what her grandma had so wisely said to her. "Look with your heart, Tula."

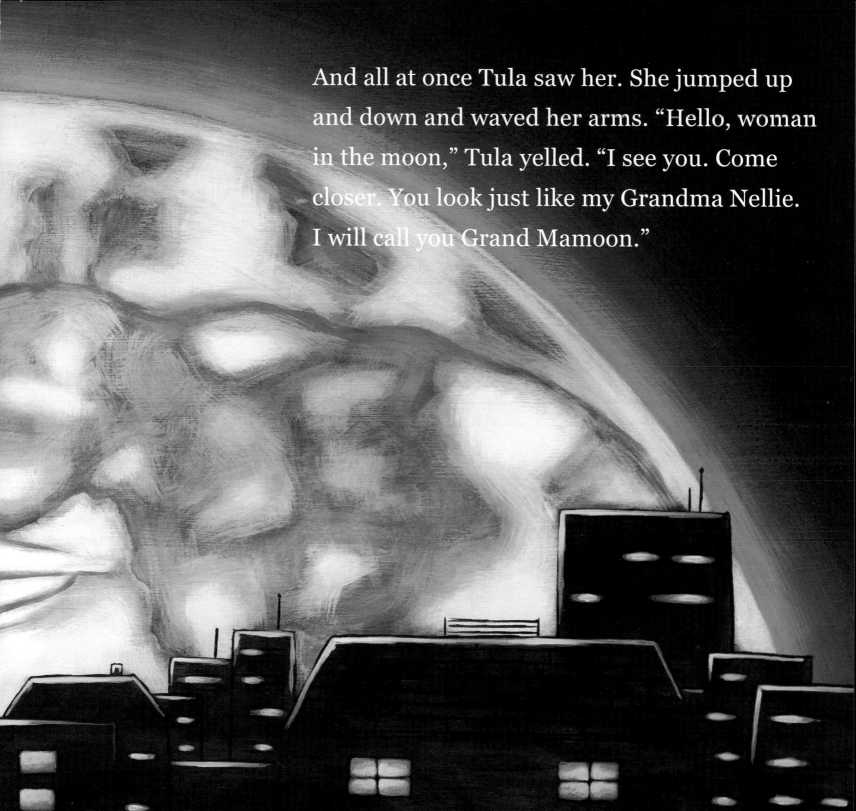

And all at once Tula saw her. She jumped up and down and waved her arms. "Hello, woman in the moon," Tula yelled. "I see you. Come closer. You look just like my Grandma Nellie. I will call you Grand Mamoon."

The next morning Tula woke up early. She had a very big idea. She drew pictures and colored on cards. She cut and pasted and worked very hard. Then she packed up her knapsack, went down to the lobby of her apartment house and put a special invitation into the mailbox of every family in the building.

You are
Invited to a
Surprise Party
tonight* at
6 O'clock
In honor of
my Grandma

At six o'clock everyone arrived for the surprise party. Tula led them all out to the terrace. "Quiet everyone," Tula hushed. Just then, Grand Mamoon began to rise high above the city. "Look," Tula yelled. "There she is shining bright. She's watching over us tonight." "What do you see, Tula? Where is your grandma?" everyone asked. "Up in the sky," Tula pointed. But no one could see what Tula saw. She held up the picture of her grandma and pointed at the moon.

"There she is. See her hair! See her nose!"

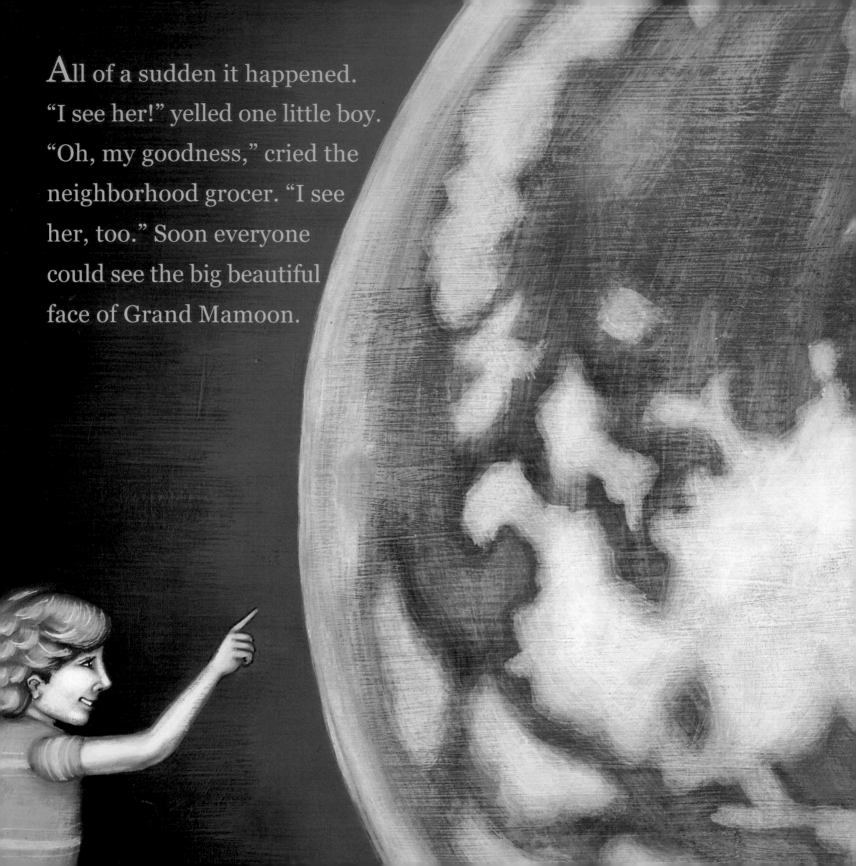

All of a sudden it happened.
"I see her!" yelled one little boy.
"Oh, my goodness," cried the
neighborhood grocer. "I see
her, too." Soon everyone
could see the big beautiful
face of Grand Mamoon.

Everybody sang and danced under the light of Grand Mamoon. Tula's family and all the neighbors shouted out greetings to her. Tom, from the music shop, played a moon song on his didgeridoo. Another neighbor with a drum pounded out a moon beat from Africa.

The news of Tula's Grand Mamoon party spread far beyond the city. Before long, children from all over Village Earth were celebrating the beauty and wonder of this ancient magical way of seeing Grand Mamoon.

Tula still misses her Grandma Nellie, but every time she looks up and sees Grand Mamoon she knows she's being watched over.

To this day, Grand Mamoon watches over all the children of Village Earth. And you can see her too, just like Tula. When the moon is full, go outside, look at the pictures of Grand Mamoon in this book and then look up at the moon.

See her hair!

See her nose!

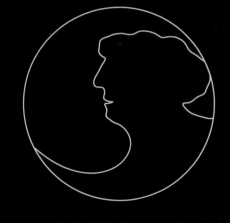

She will always appear for you!